Samuel French Acting Edition

C000302802

How to Eat Like a Child

And Other Lessons in Not Being a Grown-up

Book by
Delia Ephron, John Forster, and
Judith Kahan

Music & Lyrics by
John Forster

Based on the Book by
Delia Ephron

SAMUELFRENCH.COM   SAMUELFRENCH.CO.UK

FOR PRODUCTION ENQUIRIES

UNITED STATES AND CANADA
Info@SamuelFrench.com
1-866-598-8449

UNITED KINGDOM AND EUROPE
Plays@SamuelFrench.co.uk
020-7255-4302

Each title is subject to availability from Samuel French, depending
upon country of performance. Please be aware that HOW TO EAT
LIKE A CHILD may not be licensed by Samuel French in your territory.
Professional and amateur producers should contact the nearest Samuel
French office or licensing partner to verify availability.

MUSIC USE NOTE

Licensees are solely responsible for obtaining formal written permission from copyright owners to use copyrighted music in the performance of this play and are strongly cautioned to do so. If no such permission is obtained by the licensee, then the licensee must use only original music that the licensee owns and controls. Licensees are solely responsible and liable for all music clearances and shall indemnify the copyright owners of the play(s) and their licensing agent, Samuel French, against any costs, expenses, losses and liabilities arising from the use of music by licensees. Please contact the appropriate music licensing authority in your territory for the rights to any incidental music.

IMPORTANT BILLING AND CREDIT REQUIREMENTS

If you have obtained performance rights to this title, please refer to your licensing agreement for important billing and credit requirements.

In addition the following credit must be given in all programs and publicity information distributed in association with this piece:

(Name of Producer)

Presents

The Musical Play

"How to Eat Like a Child
And Other Lessons in Not Being a Grown-up"

Book by
Delia Ephron, John Forster and Judith Kahan

Music and Lyrics by
John Forster

Based on a Book by Delia Ephron

The first musical version of *How to Eat Like a Child* was produced for television as an NBC Project Peacock special, starring Dick Van Dyke, in 1981. Then, using songs from the television show, it was adapted for the stage as a musical revue to be performed exclusively by children. The first production, in New York City in 1984, was by TADA! (the Theater and Dance Alliance).

TADA! THEATER AND DANCE ALLIANCE

Produced by Janine Nina Trevens
Co-Artistic Directors: Linda Reiff & Janine Nina Trevens

presents

HOW TO EAT LIKE A CHILD
And Other Lessons in Not Being a Grown-up.

Music and Lyrics by
JOHN FORSTER

Written by
DELIA EPHRON, JOHN FORSTER
and JUDITH KAHAN

Based on the book by DELIA EPHRON

Sets by	Leon Munier
Lights by	Victor En Yu Tan
Costumes by	Patrick Jon Boylan
Musical Director	Joel Gelpe
Vocal Director	Mary Ellinger
Production Stage Manager	Elizabeth Rogers
Choreographer	Linda Reiff
Directed by	James Learned

CAST
(in alphabetical order):

Sasha Cincotta	J.P. Nair
Kim Conroy	Melonie Penrhyn
Julie Cutrer	Tweeps Phillips
Seth Granger	Serena I. Rosario
Tiyese Graves	Kirsten Sheridan
Mika Hadani	Naomi Sheridan
Chad Kraus	Sean Smith
	Antuane Thomas

BAND

Piano	Joel Gelpe
Percussion	Gary Seligson

PRODUCTION NOTES

How To Eat Like a Child, a collection of songs and sketches, is a guide to the art of being a child told by children strictly from their point of view. The revue, in one act, is divided into "lessons." The lessons are printed on title cards, which are displayed vaudeville style, stacked on an easel. Generally, though not always, as each lesson begins, a cast member removes the previous title card to reveal a new one and announces the next lesson.

The revue, as written, is for 15 children, but the number of speaking roles can be reduced by doubling up parts or expanded by dividing them up if there is a need to have more or fewer children in the production. The role of removing cards and announcing lessons can be given to children who are not performing or to one child who acts, in effect, as the MC.

CAST NOTES

The players can range in age from five to fifteen. The names of characters used here are the actual names of the children in the original show. So, in each specific production, characters should be referred to by their own names. Some notes on the players:

GEORGE is the leader, a rock 'n roller. He has to have a strong voice. ANDY is the best singer. COREY, the comedian, needn't sing well. RACHEL is very bossy, very dramatic. She has to be a good singer. REBECCA sings very little. ARLENE, KIMBERLY and PAULA, who sing "I Feel Sick" together, should be cast older, middle and younger sister, respectively. BILLY is George's sidekick. BRANDON is the youngest player.

THE CHILDREN
(in order of appearance)

COREY
RACHEL
ARLENE
JOHN
CHRISTY
KIMBERLY
DARIEN
ANDY
BRANDON
GEORGE
RICKY
BILLY
PAULA
REBECCA
SUNSHINE

THE LESSONS

Supplemental Lessons (optional)

Lesson: HOW TO BEHAVE AT SCHOOL
Lesson: HOW TO BRAG
  "The Brag Rag" .... Ricky & John

How to Eat Like a Child

And Other Lessons in Not Being a Grown-up

PROLOGUE
[MUSIC: PROLOGUE]

Dark stage. MUSIC. Spotlight will illuminate one group of kids after another. Action moves quickly. Lines of dialogue punctuate the underscoring.

COREY. (*dialing the telephone*) Hello. Is your refrigerator running? Then you'd better go and catch it.

(*He hangs up and cracks up. MUSIC. Spot now illuminates ARLENE and RACHEL. RACHEL lies on the floor reading, her legs waving in the air; ARLENE is playing with a yoyo.*)

RACHEL. Would you rather freeze to death or be burned alive?
ARLENE. Freeze to death. No wait, burned alive. No, wait—

(*MUSIC. Spot cuts over to . . .*)

JOHN. (*yelling*) Hey, Mom, watch me, watch me, watch me, watch me.

(*He stands on his head. MUSIC. Spot now picks out CHRISTY, KIMBERLY, DARIEN, and ANDY, as CHRISTY is handing a quarter of an orange to each.*)

CHRISTY. Ready? One, two, three . . .

(*They each stuff the entire orange quarter in their mouths and smile huge orange peel smiles. MUSIC. Spot now illuminates BRANDON, talking to RICKY, GEORGE, BILLY and PAULA.*)

BRANDON. Knock, knock.
GEORGE. Who's there?

11

BRANDON. Me.
GEORGE. Me who?
BRANDON. Me, Brandon. Don't you recognize me?

(*GEORGE, BILLY, RICKY, and PAULA groan. MUSIC. Spot
    now picks out REBECCA and SUNSHINE sitting next to
    each other, chewing gum. Simultaneously, they each pull
    one end of the gum out of their mouths and stretch it into a
    spaghetti-like strand. Then they attach the ends of their gum
    together. As they press the ends together . . .*)

REBECCA & SUNSHINE. Ooooooooooooooooo. Gross . . .

(*MUSIC. ANDY notices the audience for the first time, and gets
    the other kids' attention. They all huddle for a moment.
    Then GEORGE comes downstage and addresses the audi-
    ence confidentially.*)

[MUSIC NO. 1: "LIKE A CHILD"]

GEORGE.
IF YOU PROMISE NOT TO TELL,
WE'VE GOT QUITE A LOT TO TELL.
STUFF WE'RE NOT SUPPOSED TO DO,
STUFF WE SHOULD, BUT DON'T
'CAUSE IT'S TOO GROSS TO DO.
IF YOU'RE SHOCKED, DON'T YELL.
    ALL.
AND WHATEVER YOU DO, DON'T TELL.

    ARLENE.
EVERYONE HATES TURNIPS
BUT GROWNUPS ALWAYS EAT THEM.
KIDS ARE MUCH TOO SMART
TO LET A VEGETABLE DEFEAT THEM.
    RICKY.
SO YOU COULD EAT YOUR TURNIPS LIKE A GROWNUP
OR YOU COULD DROP 'EM IN YOUR NAPKIN
BEFORE THEY REACH YOUR MOUTH
AND SMUGGLE THEM TO THE GARBAGE
LIKE A CHILD.

ALL. (*with simple movements or dance steps*)
LIKE A CHILD, LIKE A CHI-CHI-CHILD,
LIKE A CHILD, LIKE A CHILD,
LIKE A CHI-CHI-CHILD.
JUST DO WHAT YOU'VE GOT TO DO
AND SMUGGLE THEM TO THE GARBAGE
LIKE A CHILD.

RACHEL.
EVERYONE'S REAL NOSY
BUT GROWNUPS TRY TO HIDE IT.
FIND A DOOR THAT SAYS . . .
  COREY. (*spoken*) "Keep Out!!"
  RACHEL. (*sings*)
. . . YOU'LL FIND A KID INSIDE IT.

(*PAULA picks up a cube to reveal ANDY behind it.*)

ANDY.
SO YOU COULD TRY TO HIDE IT LIKE A GROWNUP
OR YOU COULD RAID YOUR PARENTS' CLOSET,
GO THROUGH THEIR DRESSER DRAWERS
TO SEE WHAT YOU'LL GET FOR CHRISTMAS
LIKE A CHILD.
  ALL. (*again with simple movements*)
LIKE A CHILD, LIKE A CHI-CHI-CHILD,
LIKE A CHILD, LIKE A CHILD,
LIKE A CHI-CHI-CHILD.
JUST DO WHAT YOU'VE GOT TO DO
AND SEE WHAT YOU'LL GET FOR CHRISTMAS
LIKE A CHILD.

YOU KNOW WHAT YOU'VE GOTTA DO.
SO JUST SET ABOUT IT.
IF YA GOTTA THINK ABOUT IT
OR FRET ABOUT IT,
FORGET ABOUT IT.
  GEORGE.
EVEN IF YOU'VE GROWN UP
AND LOST YOUR EFFERVESCENCE,
DOESN'T MEAN YOU CAN'T HAVE FUN.
IT JUST MEANS YOU NEED LESSONS.

ALL.

SO YOU COULD SIT THERE THINKIN' LIKE A GROWN-UP . . .

RICKY.

. . . OR YOU COULD COME ALONG AND JOIN US,

(*The COMPANY breaks into smaller groups, each with its own playground activity — tag, somersaults, etc.*)

RACHEL.

CLOWN AROUND THE PLAYGROUND,

(*The following four lines may be spoken for greater intelligibility.*)

PAULA.

JUMP AND BUMP YOUR NOGGIN,

ANDY.

TRIP AND RIP YOUR TROUSERS,

JOHN.

LOSE YOUR MITTEN,

DARIEN.

SKIN YOUR ELBOW,

ARLENE. (*sung*)

AND START TO CRY,

ALL.

AND, FIFTEEN SECONDS LATER,
  FEEL SO HIGH,
ROAMIN' THROUGH THE WILD
LIKE A . . .

PAULA.

WE DO WHAT WE'VE GOT TO,

CHRISTY.

EVEN IF WE'RE NOT TO.

ALL.

LIKE A CHI-CHI-CHILD.

(*lots of playground activity*)

LIKE A CHI-CHI-CHILD!
YEAH!

(*Black out.*)

LESSON #1

GEORGE, holding a microphone and posing as a television

reporter, is interviewing REBECCA and COREY, D.R.
BILLY stands in front of them.

BILLY. (*clicking a movie clapper board*) How to Eat Like a
Child, Part 1. (*Exits.*)

GEORGE. Hello there. We're eating potatoes with Rebecca and
her brother, Corey. Rebecca, tell us, how do you handle mashed
potatoes?

REBECCA. Well, George, first I pat the potatoes flat. (*demonstrates*) I dig three or four holes and fill them with gravy to make
gravy lakes. (*does so*) Then, with my fork, I carve rivers between the lakes and watch the gravy flow between them. (*does
so.*) I decorate the whole thing with peas.

GEORGE. When do you eat the potatoes?

REBECCA. I don't.

GEORGE. Corey, what about French fries? Are they eaten?

COREY. Definitely. But you have to start by waving one French
fry in the air for emphasis, like this. (*He demonstrates.
GEORGE moves back a little to get out of the way.*) Pretend to
conduct an orchestra. (*does so, humming some music*) Then . . .
place four French fries in your mouth at once (*does so*) and
chew. Turn to your sister and open your mouth. (*Does so; RE-
BECCA recoils.*)

GEORGE. (*peering into COREY's mouth*) That's disgusting.

COREY. (*pleased*) That's the point.

(*Black out.*)

[MUSIC NO. 1A: PLAYOFF]

LESSON #2

Lights up C.S. *Cubes are arranged into three parallel beds with
blanket covers. Feet of beds face* DS. *REBECCA, playing
"the mother," enters.*

REBECCA. Hurry up. The bus will be here in ten minutes.
Don't forget—you have that big test today. (*Exits.*)

JOHN. (*removing previous title card*) How to Stay Home From School. (*Exits.*)

[MUSIC NO. 2: "I FEEL SICK"]

(*NOTE: Each girl should remain motionless under her covers and not visible to the audience until she makes her first singing "entrance." The sisters should clearly be faking their illnesses.*)

ARLENE. (*sitting up in bed #1*)
I FEEL SICK.
AWFUL SICK.
TOO SICK TO DO
ARITH . . .
(*She coughs.*)
. . . METIC.

IT'S A COLD IN MY HEAD.
I BELONG IN MY BED.
WHAT I NEED
IS A DOSE OF SAINT JOSEPH'S ASPIRIN.
(*She sniffles, wipes nose with hand.*)
AND THOUGH I HATE TO MISS THAT TEST,
WHAT I REALLY NEED IS REST
'CAUSE—

I FEEL SICK.
  KIMBERLY. (*pops up in bed #2*)
ME, TOO.
  ARLENE.
AWFUL SICK.
  KIMBERLY.
YOU SAID IT.
  ARLENE.
TOO SICK . . .
  KIMBERLY.
SHE COUGHED . . .
  ARLENE.
. . . TO DO . . .
  KIMBERLY.
. . . ON ME . . .

(*ARLENE coughs loudly.*)

AND SPREAD IT.

ARLENE.
IT'S A COLD.
    KIMBERLY.
IT'S A GRIP.
    ARLENE.
IT'S A FLU.
    KIMBERLY.
OH YES.
    ARLENE.
WHERE YA WHEEZE,
    KIMBERLY.
AND YA SNEEZE,
    ARLENE.
AH-CAH-CHOO!
    KIMBERLY.
GOD BLESS.
    ARLENE & KIMBERLY.
AND YA KNOW WHAT YA NEED
IS A DOSE OF SAINT JOSEPH'S ASPIRIN.

(*Both sniffle and wipe noses with hands.*)

    ARLENE. (*pointing to arm*)
YOU SEE THIS DOT?
IT'S A MEASLE.
    KIMBERLY.
ON TOP OF A NASTY FLU.
    ARLENE. (*points to "swollen gland"*)
AND THIS BUMP
    KIMBERLY.
WHERE?
    ARLENE.
COULD BE A MUMP.
    KIMBERLY.
IT'S A MUMP.
    PAULA. (*pops up in bed #3*)
I'VE GOT A MUMP, TOO

I FEEL SICK.
    KIMBERLY.
SICK.

PAULA.
SICK.
AWFUL . . .
KIMBERLY.
AWFUL . . .
PAULA.
SICK.
ARLENE.
IT'S CONTAGIOUS.
KIMBERLY.
PHLEGM.
PAULA.
IT'S AN EPIDEMIC.
KIMBERLY.
RIGHT!
ARLENE.
AND IT STRIKES . . .
ALL.
ALL AGES.

PAULA.
IT'S A BUG.
ARLENE.
IT'S A PLAGUE.
KIMBERLY.
IT'S A RARE DISEASE.
PAULA.
IT'S A GRIP.
ARLENE.
IT'S A FLU.
KIMBERLY.
WHERE YA BURN
PAULA.
AND FREEZE.
ALL.
AND WE'RE SURE THAT THE CURE
IS A DOSE OF SAINT JOSEPH'S ASPIRIN.

(*They all three sniffle and wipe noses with lengths of arms.*)

ARLENE.
WE'LL ALL FEEL BETTER TOMORROW.

KIMBERLY.
YES, THAT WE CAN SAFELY SAY.

PAULA.
WE'LL FEEL FINE THE REST OF OUR LIVES

ALL.
IF YA LET US SUFFER TODAY.

(*INSTRUMENTAL, during which the kids stand up in their beds and diagnose each other, sticking out tongues, saying "Ah," testing reflexes, searching for possible measles, etc.*)

ARLENE. (*examining PAULA's neck*)
I HAVE FOUND MORE DOTS!

PAULA. (*alarmed*)
BUT I DON'T NEED SHOTS.

ALL.
JUST A DOSE OF SAINT JOSEPH'S

PAULA.
ASPIRIN—

KIMBERLY.
ASPIRIN—

ARLENE.
ASPIRIN.

(*All now with GREAT SUFFERING.*)

PAULA. (*collapsing in bed*)
OW—

KIMBERLY. (*collapsing*)
EE—

ARLENE. (*collapsing*)
OH—

(*The suffering grows as they writhe on their beds in pain.*)

PAULA.
AH!

OW—

KIMBERLY.
EE—

ARLENE.
OH—

PAULA.
AH!

OW—
   KIMBERLY.
EE—
   ARLENE.
OH—
   ALL.
AH!
   PAULA.
OW—
   KIMBERLY.
EE—
   ARLENE.
OH—
   ALL.
AH!
ASPIRIN!
(*rationally*)
SO WHAT'S THE USE OF GOING WHEN
THE NURSE WOULD ONLY
   SEND US HOME AGAIN?

(*REBECCA re-enters.*)

   REBECCA. I know you're not feeling very well, but I'm sure
you'll feel better once you get to school.
   ARLENE. (*sings*)
OH RATS!
   KIMBERLY.
OH NUTS!
   PAULA.
OH SHUCKS!
   ARLENE.
BUT WHY?
   ALL.
OH, WELL.
IT WAS WORTH A TRY.

(*Black out.*)

LESSON #3

   ANDY. (*removing the previous title card*) How to Ride in a
Car. (*Exits.*)

(At C.S. are DARIEN, COREY, REBECCA, RACHEL, BILLY, and BRANDON. This lesson can be presented in choral speaking-style or staged to suggest the front and back seats of a car.)

DARIEN. Insist that you don't have to go to the bathroom. If your mother points out that sometimes you think you don't have to go and then it turns out that you do, claim that you just went. Then have this conversation with your sister.

(COREY and REBECCA in rapid exchange:)

COREY. Dibs on the front seat.
REBECCA. I want it. You always get it.
COREY. You had it last time.
REBECCA. *You* had it last time.
COREY. I did not.
REBECCA. Did too.
COREY. Did not. What a liar.
REBECCA. I am not a liar. Mom, he called me a liar.

RACHEL. Your mother will say that she can't stand it another minute—no one is sitting in front.
DARIEN. Once you're in the car, draw an imaginary line down the back of the front seat, across the floor and up the back seat. Tell your sister not to cross the line, saying,
COREY. Stay on your own side—I don't want your cooties.
BRANDON. Ask if you're almost there yet.
DARIEN. Shortly after the car leaves the driveway, announce that you have to go to the bathroom, and deny kicking your sister.
RACHEL. Tell your mother that she's driving over the speed limit. Tell her that her seat belt isn't fastened. Tell her that a person's always supposed to drive with both hands on the wheel. Tell her that she really shouldn't smoke; it's bad for her.
BRANDON. Ask if you're almost there yet.
BILLY. Good grief. Now your sister thinks she is getting carsick. Make a horrible face. Like this: *(COREY makes an atrocious face.)*
BILLY. Or this: *(DARIEN makes an atrocious face.)* Say, "Euuu, she's always getting sick. P.U." Holding your nose say, the car is going to smell re-volting. Say to her—
COREY. Don't throw up on me.

DARIEN. Tell your mom it's stupid to take her anywhere since she practically barfs the second she gets in the car. Whisper to your sister—

COREY. Want a sandwich, hee hee hee.

RACHEL. When she clutches her stomach and tells your mom to make you stop, say,

COREY. (*innocently*) All I said was, 'Want a sandwich.'

BRANDON. Ask if you're almost there yet.

DARIEN. Lean back against the seat. Close your eyes. Think about your sister. Yuck, she is disgusting. Open your eyes and look at her. Swear that you'll never talk to her again. Ever. More than anything wish that you were an only child.

BRANDON. Ask if you're almost there yet.

(*Cross fade to . . .*)

LESSON #4

COREY. (*on the telephone*) Hello. I'm taking a survey. Have you ever eaten peanut butter and amatta? What's amatta? I don't know. What's amatta with you? (*He hangs up and shrieks with laughter. Cross fade to . . .*)

LESSON #5

SUNSHINE. (*removing previous title card*) How to Practice the Violin.

(*JOHN is at a music stand. ARLENE enters.*)

ARLENE. (*as "the mother"*) I'm sorry, John. You can't go out to play unless you finish practicing. (*Exits.*)

(*JOHN picks up violin and starts metronome ticking. He plays.*)

[MUSIC NO. 3: "THE JOLLY BUCCANEERS"]*

---

*(NOTE: The violin part is simple enough to be learned by a non-violinist with just a few hours' practice. A violin teacher's guidance is recommended. As a last resort, the violin playing can be mimed while the pianist plays the musical line. In

JOHN. (*glumly*)
BOY, IS THIS A STUPID PIECE OF MUSIC.
WHY'S IT CALLED "THE JOLLY BUCCANEERS"?
IT DOESN'T MAKE ME THINK
 OF SHIPS OR PIRATES.
IT MAKES ME WANT TO HOLD MY EARS.

DEVO IS MUSIC.
SO ARE *THE CLASH*.
KISS IS MUSIC.
THIS IS TRASH.

WISH I HAD A RICKENBACKER TWELVE-STRING.
(*Guitar chord—audience hears what JOHN imagines.*)
NOT THIS DUMB OL' CREEPY VIOLIN.
(*Guitar fill*)
AN INSTRUMENT DOES NOT BECOME AN
 INSTRUMENT
UNTIL YOU PLUG IT IN.

(*Rock music fills the air. JOHN undergoes a complete physical
 transformation into a macho rock star. Besides turning up
 his collar or ripping open his shirt, he struts, swaggers and
 gyrates as he plays to an imaginary audience of adoring
 fans, using the violin as a Heavy Metal guitarist would use a
 guitar. The Lights pulsate during the instrumental.*
*Suddenly it's over . . . the guitar sound fades; the metronome
 sound reappears. JOHN dejectedly goes back to practicing
 the violin.*
Music and Lights slowly fade.)

LESSON #6

KIMBERLY. (*removing previous title card*) How to Express an
Opinion.

---

that case, the violin strings should be replaced with twine so that no sound comes
out.
 If a sound system—or even a beatbox—is available a pre-recorded rock music
tape can be used. If a guitarist is available, he/she can improvise the part, playing
the heaviest riffs they know. If neither a sound system or a guitarist is available,
the song can be omitted from the show.)

(*CHRISTY steps up to a podium and clears her throat. The others, except GEORGE, BILLY, and BRANDON, form an appreciative audience. CHRISTY begins quietly, almost clinically, but she adds emotion gradually and finishes with grand oratorical flourishes.*)

CHRISTY. Yucky . . . Gross . . . Dis-gusting . . . Ugh!! . . . Scuzzy . . . Sick . . . Sickening . . . Hideola . . . Creepy . . . Icky . . . Obnoxious . . . Creeps . . . Crummy . . . Vomitrocious.

(*She bows. The others applaud. All exit but COREY, who removes the title card to reveal the next one, "How to Beg for a Dog," but he does not read it.*)

LESSON #7

GEORGE enters.

GEORGE. (*to audience*) Persuading your parents to let you have a dog is one of the toughest things you'll ever have to do. But it can be done. Here's how my brother and I finally did it.

(*BILLY enters leading a dog, played by BRANDON, wearing cocker spaniel ears.*)

GEORGE. (*continued*) We found an actual dog up for adoption. We brought him to our house and stationed him by the fireplace. Then, when our parents came home . . .

[MUSIC NO. 4: "SAY YES"]

. . . We went to work.

(*GEORGE and BILLY work the audience with the clockwork precision of a vaudeville team. NOTE: Utter sincerity is important—even in the dog.*)

GEORGE. (*speaking in rhythm*)
OH MY GOSH! IS THAT A DOG?
    BILLY.
YES, THAT'S A DOG.

GEORGE.
WHOSE DOG IS IT?
BILLY.
THAT'S THE DOG THAT JERRY'S FAMILY
WON'T LET HIM KEEP.
GEORGE.
YOU MEAN TO SAY HE'S HOMELESS?
BILLY.
YES, HE'S HOMELESS.
GEORGE.
WHAT A TRAGEDY!
BILLY.
IF THEY DON'T FIND A HOME FOR HIM
THEY'LL HAVE HIM PUT TO SLEEP.
GEORGE.
OH—NO!
WELL, HOW MUCH IS THAT DOGGIE?
BILLY.
HE'S FREE.
GEORGE.
DID YOU SAY FREE?
BILLY.
I SAID FREE.
GEORGE.
I CAN'T BELIEVE IT.
BILLY.
WELL, IT'S TRUE.
GEORGE.
THAT'S GREAT.
AND WHEN IS HE AVAILABLE?
BILLY.
IMMEDIATELY AVAILABLE.
GEORGE.
RIGHT NOW?
BILLY.
RIGHT NOW.
GEORGE.
OH MY GOSH! IT'S FATE.

GEORGE & BILLY. (*singing and doing a simple vaudeville step*)
THIS DOG IS FREE
AND SO ARE WE.

WHAT A SENSIBLE ADDITION TO THE FAMILY.
HE'S ADORABLE, AVAILABLE AND ODORLESS.
DON'T BREAK OUR HEARTS.
SAY YES.

GEORGE. That performance alone will not get you a dog, but it's a start. Now you've got to come up with practical arguments. For example: (*speaking in rhythm*)
NOW HOW IS HE AT BURGLARS?
  BILLY.
HE'S EXCELLENT AT BURGLARS.
  GEORGE.
DOES HE SCARE 'EM?
  BILLY.
HE'S AS SCARY AS A JUNGLE CAT.
  GEORGE.
AND HOW IS HE WITH CHILDREN?
IS HE GENTLE?
  BILLY.
VERY GENTLE.
  GEORGE.
WOULD HE KEEP 'EM OUT OF DANGER?
  BILLY.
HE'S A SPECIALIST AT THAT.

GEORGE & BILLY. (*singing and dancing*)
THIS DOG IS SMART.
THIS DOG HAS HEART.
YOU COULD HITCH HIM UP AND HAVE HIM PULL
  YOUR SHOPPING CART.
HE'S AS WONDERFUL WITH CHILDREN AS A
  GOVERNESS.
THIS DOG'S A SAINT.
SAY YES.

IF YOU SAY YES
INSTEAD OF NO,
HE'S SURE TO COME IN HANDY.
LIKE WHEN YOU'RE STRANDED IN THE SNOW
  BILLY.
HE'LL COME THROUGH WITH THE BRANDY.

GEORGE. (*speaking in rhythm*)
NOW WHO IS GONNA WALK HIM?
  BILLY.
US!
  GEORGE.
WHO WILL TEACH HIM TRICKS?
  BILLY.
US!
  GEORGE.
WHO IS GONNA FEED HIM?
  BILLY.
US!
  GEORGE.
WHO WILL CHECK FOR TICKS?
  BILLY. (*spoken*) You.
  GEORGE. *And* you.
  BILLY. *And* me.
  GEORGE. Right. (*speaking in rhythm*)
AND MOM AND DAD WON'T HAVE TO LIFT A FINGER?
  BILLY.
WE SWEAR.
  GEORGE.
WE'LL BE SO RESPONSIBLE THAT
  NOBODY WILL EVEN KNOW HE'S THERE.
  GEORGE & BILLY. (*singing*)
OUR FINGERS ITCH
TO PET THIS DOG.
WE NEEDED HIM THE MOMENT THAT WE MET THIS
  DOG.
AND WE'LL NAG AND NAG AND NAG UNTIL WE GET
  THIS DOG.
  GEORGE.
LOOK AT THAT FACE!
  BILLY.
LOOK AT THAT LEG!
  GEORGE.
COME ON, ROVER, BEG!

(*BRANDON "begs."*)

  GEORGE & BILLY. (*really pouring it on*)
IT MIGHT TAKE THREATS.

IT MIGHT TAKE TEARS.
IT'S GONNA TAKE SOME PATIENCE
'CAUSE IT MIGHT TAKE YEARS.
   GEORGE.
BUT ONE DAY YOU'LL FINALLY WEAR 'EM DOWN
AND THEN—
   GEORGE & BILLY.
THREE CHEERS.

(*BRANDON barks.*)

THEY'RE GONNA SAY
"ALL RIGHT."
"OKAY."
"ANYTHING YOU SAY."
THEY'LL SAY—
"YES, YES, YES, YES,
YES!"

(*BRANDON barks. Black out.*)

LESSON #8

DARIEN. (*removing previous title card*) How to Play. (*Exits.*)

(*RACHEL, RICKY, CHRISTY, SUNSHINE, and REBECCA deliver this lesson in a choral speaking style.*)

RACHEL. Wander around the house trying different seats. Say, "I'm so bored, I've never been so bored, I'm going to die of boredom, there's nothing to do."

RICKY. Your mother will suggest all sorts of games that you might like to play. Say, "Nah, I don't feel like it" to every one.

CHRISTY. Open the refrigerator, look inside, close the refrigerator.

SUNSHINE. Decide to form a club. Appoint yourself president. Think about the kids in the class who you do not want to join because they have no personality at all. Call them up and announce that you're organizing a club and they can't join.

RACHEL. Fly a kite out of your bedroom window.

REBECCA. Look in your mother's dresser drawers.

RICKY. Ask for the keys to the car. You want to sit in it and listen to the radio.

CHRISTY. Open the refrigerator, look inside, close the refrigerator.

RACHEL. Decide to make chocolate pudding. Rip open the package so that half the mix lands on the saucepan and the other half lands on the floor.

CHRISTY. Spread it around with your feet so the mix blends in with the linoleum print. Stir the pudding and when it doesn't thicken fast enough, say "It's probably done anyway."

RICKY. On your way out of the kitchen, run and slide on the mix-covered floor.

SUNSHINE. Throw raisins in the air and try to catch them in your mouth. Miss. Throw raisins in your friend's mouth while he throws them into yours. Miss. Put raisins on your face and let the dog lick them off until your mother comes out and says,

RACHEL. (*as "the mom"*) Don't let the dog lick your face, he has germs.

REBECCA. Put your chin in a glass and move it around the table. (*She demonstrates.*)

RICKY. Then, pretending to be a TV newscaster, use the glass as a microphone.

REBECCA. (*talking into a glass*) Good evening, everyone. It's Saturday at the house and there's not much happening. I'm sitting at the table drinking juice.

CHRISTY. Your mother will walk in and say—

RACHEL. (*sternly*) Have you been looking in my dresser drawers?

CHRISTY. Be shocked.

REBECCA. (*shocked*) No, Mom, why?!

SUNSHINE. Your mother will say—

RACHEL. I don't mind if you did, I only mind if you lie to me.

CHRISTY. Be even more shocked.

REBECCA. (*even more shocked*) No, Mom, honest!

(*Segue to . . .*)

LESSON #9

Rest of company enters. BRANDON removes the previous title card.

ALL. How to Understand Your Parents.

(*KIMBERLY plays "Everymom;" DARIEN plays "Everydad." They stand in front of the rest of the group.*)

[MUSIC NO. 5: "MEANS NO"]

(The tone should be stern and serious, the staging static and ora-torio-like. The only movement should be the kids' sneaking DS. behind the "parents," later in the song.)

RICKY.
PARENTS TALK A SPECIAL LANGUAGE.
LET US DEMONSTRATE.
    KIMBERLY & DARIEN.
WE'LL SAY THINGS A PARENT SAYS.
    ALL OTHERS.
AND WE'LL TRANSLATE.
    KIMBERLY.
"WE'LL SEE . . ."
    ALL OTHERS.
. . . MEANS "NO."
    DARIEN.
"NOT NOW . . ."
    ALL OTHERS.
. . . MEANS "NO."
    KIMBERLY.
"ASK YOUR FATHER . . ."
    ALL OTHERS.
. . . MEANS "NO."
    DARIEN.
"ASK YOUR MOTHER . . ."
    ALL OTHERS.
. . . MEANS "NO."
    KIMBERLY.
"MAYBE WHEN YOU'RE OLDER . . ."
    ALL OTHERS.
. . . MEANS "NO."
    DARIEN.
"WE'LL DISCUSS IT LATER . . ."
    ALL OTHERS.
. . . MEANS "NO."
    KIMBERLY.
"IS YOUR BED MADE?"
    ALL OTHERS. *(beginning to move DS. toward "parents")*
"NO!"

DARIEN.
"IS YOUR ROOM CLEAN?"
    ALL OTHERS.
"NO!"
    KIMBERLY & DARIEN.
"WHAT DO YOU THINK?"
    ALL OTHERS.
"NO, NO, NO!"

(*Now surrounding the parents.*)

WHY IS "NO" THE ONLY THING
A PARENT CAN EXPRESS?
THERE OUGHT TO BE
AS MANY WAYS OF SAYING . . .
(*very sweetly*)
"YES!"

(*Lights Fade.*)

LESSON #10

Lights up D.R. . . . .

COREY. (*on the telephone*) Hello, is this the supermarket? Do you have pigs feet? Then how do you get your shoes on? (*He hangs up and cracks up. Segue to . . .*)

LESSON #11

BILLY, D.L., *is in front of GEORGE and DARIEN.*

BILLY. (*clicking clapper board*) How to Eat Like a Child, Part 2. (*Exits.*)

GEORGE. (*as the interviewer*) We're at McDonald's with Darien, who will show us how to drink a milkshake. Darien, where do you start?
DARIEN. (*demonstrates as he speaks*) Place the straw in the shake and suck. When the shake just reaches your mouth, place

a finger over the top of the straw . . . (*He holds up the straw.*)
And the shake just stays there.

GEORGE. That's neat.

DARIEN. Then lift the bottom end of the straw to your mouth,
(*He does.*) release your finger, and boom, down comes the shake.

GEORGE. Amazing.

DARIEN. It is, isn't it? Well, just keep going 'til you get near
the bottom and then blow bubbles that come up to the top of the
glass. (*He does so.*) When your father says he's had just about
enough, (*big smile*) get a stomach ache.

(*Black out.*)

[MUSIC NO. 5A: PLAYOFF]

LESSON #12

Lights up C.S. *CHRISTY, as "the mother," sweeps, dusts, and
does household chores during first half of song. SUNSHINE
is the child.*

CHRISTY. I'm sorry. I don't have time to take you to the store
right now. You'll have to walk. (*She continues with her chores,
and ignores SUNSHINE's pleading.*)

[MUSIC NO. 6: "WHY SHOULD A KID HAVE TO WALK?"]*

ANDY. (*removing the previous title card*) How to Deal With
Injustice.

SUNSHINE. (*following her mother around*)
WHY SHOULD A KID WHO HAS RUN OUT OF GUM
HAVE TO BEG FOR A RIDE TO THE STORE?
WHICH BY CAR IS JUST MINUTES AWAY
BUT ON FOOT COULD TAKE HALF OF THE DAY.

---

*NOTE: This song has a vocal range of an octave and a fourth, which can be dif-
ficult for an unchanged voice. It should therefore be assigned to the best singer
available.

AND WHY CAN A GROWN-UP ZOOM OFF IN THE CAR
TO A PARTY THAT'S RIGHT DOWN THE BLOCK?
AND WHEN EVEN YOUR PET
GETS A RIDE TO THE VET,
OH WHY SHOULD A KID HAVE TO WALK?

(*CHRISTY exits. SUNSHINE sings directly to the audience.*)

WANDERING THROUGH THE TRAFFIC,
PROBABLY GETTING LOST.
PROBABLY GETTING HIT BY A CAR,
BIT BY A DOG,
CHOKED BY EXHAUST.

AND ANOTHER THING:
WHY SHOULD A KID HAVE TO WHEEDLE AND PLEAD
FOR A RIDE THAT SHE REALLY DESERVES?
WE'D BE BACK BEFORE TEN MINUTES PASS.
I'D BE HAPPY TO PAY FOR THE GAS.

IN THIS LAND WE HAVE
TAXIS AND TRAINS,
HELICOPTERS AND PLANES.
YOU CAN FLY THROUGH THE SKY LIKE A HAWK.
WE HAVE TUGS AND CANOES.
WE HAVE B-52'S.
SO WHY SHOULD A KID HAVE TO WEAR OUT HER
   SHOES?
OH WHY SHOULD A KID HAVE TO WALK
AND WALK
AND WALK
AND WALK
AND WALK?

(*She trudges off stage. Lights fade.*)

LESSON #13

REBECCA. (*removing previous title card*) How to Hang Up the
Telephone.

(*ARLENE and KIMBERLY, each reclining in her own area, talk on the phone.*)

ARLENE. Goodbye.
KIMBERLY. 'Bye.
ARLENE. Are you still there?
KIMBERLY. Yeah. Why didn't you hang up?
ARLENE. Why didn't you?
KIMBERLY. I was waiting for you.
ARLENE. I was waiting for *you.* You go first.
KIMBERLY. No, you first.
ARLENE. No, you first.
KIMBERLY. No, you first.
ARLENE. Okay, I know. I'll count to three and we'll both hang up at the same time. Ready? One, two, three, 'bye.
KIMBERLY. 'Bye.
ARLENE. (*after a pause*) Are you still there?
KIMBERLY. Yeah.
ARLENE. Why didn't you?
KIMBERLY. What do you mean, me?
ARLENE. Okay, do it again. This time for real. One, two, two-and-a-half, two-and-three-quarters, three. 'Bye.
KIMBERLY. 'Bye.
ARLENE. Hello.
KIMBERLY. Hello.
ARLENE. Are you still there?
KIMBERLY. Yeah.

(*Lights fade quickly.*)

LESSON #14

GEORGE. (*removing previous title card*) How to Wait. (*Exits.*)

(*Lights up c.s. PAULA, sitting on a bench, is bundled in a parka. By her side is a backpack and thermos.*)

[MUSIC NO. 7: "WAITING, WAITING"]

PAULA. (*matter-of-factly*)
SCHOOL IS OVER
SO HERE I WAIT . . . (*She sighs.*)
FOR MY MOTHER,
WHO, AS USUAL, IS LATE.

WAITING, WAITING
FOR A DISORGANIZED ADULT.
NOTHING'S MORE EXASPERATING
OR MORE DIFFICULT.

(*She looks both ways.*)

I BET I PROB'BLY COULD HAVE CRAWLED HOME BY
    NOW.
I NEED A DRINK.
(*She opens her thermos.*)
DOES CHOC'LATE MILK COME FROM A CHOCOLATE
    COW?
IT MAKES YA THINK.
(*She pours; it's empty.*)
OH NO!
ALL GONE!
NOTHIN' MAKES YA THIRSTIER THAN . . .

WAITING, WAITING.
MAYBE I SHOULD HAVE PITCHED A TENT.
PRETTY SOON I'LL HAVE PNEUMONIA
OR (*She crosses her legs.*) AN ACCIDENT.

(*She stands, suddenly very worried. NOTE: The child might try
    imagining that lions are really loose to help create the stage
    reality of being in a dangerous environment.*)

WHAT IF SHE CLEAN FORGOT SHE SAID HALF PAST
    TWO
AND NEVER SHOWED?
WHAT IF A LION THAT ESCAPED FROM THE ZOO
CAME DOWN THE ROAD?

I'D DISAPPEAR

WITHOUT A CLUE.
AND THERE'D BE NOTHIN' ANYBODY COULD DO.
OH MOM, OH MOM, PLEASE HURRY, MOM.
IT'S NOT EASY TO STAY CALM WHILE . . .

(*really panicked*)
WAITING, WAITING,
MY LEG IS ASLEEP, MY THERMOS DRY.
(*suddenly parched*)
WATER! WATER!
WHO SAYS THAT I'M TOO OLD TO CRY?

LIONS ARE LOOSE AND I AM STUCK
ALL BY MYSELF, A SITTING DUCK.
OH HURRY UP, HURRY UP,
HURRY UP, HURRY UP,
MOM! (*Sound of a car horn. PAULA instantly returns from panic to exasperation.*)

(*spoken indignantly to off-stage mom*) It's about time.

(*She gathers her thermos and backpack and exits. Black out.*)

Lesson #15

BILLY, D.L., *stands in front of GEORGE and BRANDON.*

BILLY. (*clicking a clapper board*) How to Eat Like a Child, Part 3. (*Exits.*)

GEORGE. (*as the interviewer*) We've asked Brandon to discuss his approach to eating animal crackers. The reason we've asked Brandon is because mainly little kids eat them. No offense, Brandon, but pretty much as soon as you know anything, you move might on to Oreos.

BRANDON. I like Oreos.

GEORGE. (*condescendingly*) Good. (*winks at audience*) Now, why don't you take an animal cracker. What part do you eat first?

BRANDON. The legs. (*He bites them off.*)
GEORGE. Then?
BRANDON. The head. (*He bites it off.*)
GEORGE. And then?
BRANDON. The body. (*He eats it.*)
GEORGE. Suppose you felt like eating the head first?
BRANDON. (*matter-of-factly*) You can't.

(*Black out.*)

[MUSIC NO. 7A: PLAYOFF]

(NOTE: Optional Supplemental Lessons—See page 51—can be inserted at this point.)

LESSON #16

Lights up D.R.

COREY. (*on the telephone*) Hello? Is this Kentucky Fried Chicken? How large are your breasts? (*He hangs up and cracks up. Black out.*)

LESSON #17

REBECCA removes the previous title card to reveal the next one, "How to Torture Your Sister," and exits.
A team of four or more "brothers" tortures a team of four or more "sisters." Each BROTHER uses his SISTER to demonstrate the torture under discussion. Actions are in unison. As MUSICAL VAMP begins, we hear teasing from the BROTHERS and protests from the SISTERS.

[MUSIC NO. 8: "HOW TO TORTURE YOUR SISTER"]

(*NOTE: It is important to remember that all the brothers' tortures are psychological in nature. Actual physical violence in the staging of this number will not be funny.*)

SISTER #1. (*spoken*) Stop it!
SISTER #2. I'm telling.
SISTER #3. That hurts.
SISTER #4. Stop that. It isn't funny.
BROTHERS. (*singing*)
HOW TO TORTURE YOUR SISTER
IS A VERY FINE ART.
F'RINSTANCE, RIGHT OFF THE BAT
YOU SHOULD TELL HER SHE'S FAT.
THAT'S A GOOD PLACE TO START.
WHEN SHE CALLS UP HER BEST FRIEND,
BUTT RIGHT INTO THEIR CHAT . . .
SISTERS. (*on the telephone*)
HOW ARE YOU?
BROTHERS. (*mimicking*)
"HOW ARE YOU?"
SISTERS.
SO WHAT'S NEW?
BROTHERS. (*mimicking*)
"SO WHAT'S NEW?"
SISTERS.
THAT'S MY BROTHER. HE'S A JERK.
BROTHERS.
"THAT'S MY BROTHER. HE'S A JERK."
SISTERS.
CUT IT OUT!
BROTHERS.
"CUT IT OUT!"
SISTERS.
I SAID STOP!
BROTHERS.
"I SAID STOP!"
SISTERS.
STOP IT!
BROTHERS.
"STOP IT!"
SISTERS.
STOP IT!
BROTHERS.
"STOP IT!"
SISTERS.
STAHHHHHHHHHHHHHHHHP!

BROTHERS.
. . . 'N STUFF LIKE THAT.

(*gleefully, with an exuberant but simple Latin dance step—rhumba, conga, etc.*)
THAT'S HOW TO TORTURE YOUR SISTER.
THAT'S HOW TO TORTURE HER GOOD.

(*Each BROTHER picks up a jelly doughnut.*)
   BROTHER #1.
SISTERS LOVE JELLY DOUGHNUTS.
THEY COULD EAT THEM ALL DAY.
   BROTHER #4.
TO GET SISTERS TO GO NUTS,
START EATING DOUGHNUTS.
THEN TURN AND SAY:
   BROTHER #3.
"DON'T YOU WISH THAT YOU HAD SOME?
(*SISTERS' mouths water.*)
WELL PERHAPS I'LL BE KIND.
I'LL BREAK THIS ONE IN TWO.
HERE A BIG PIECE FOR YOU.
IT'S INCREDIBLY . . .
   ALL BROTHERS.
YUM YUM YUM YUM—
(*The SISTERS are panting.*)
   BROTHER #3. (*spoken*)
I'VE CHANGED MY MIND.
(*The SISTERS are furious.*)
   ALL BROTHERS. (*sing*)
THAT'S HOW TO TORTURE YOUR SISTER.
LA-LA-LA-LA.
THAT'S HOW TO TORTURE HER GOOD.

(*Each BROTHER picks up a small bowl of Jello.*)
   BROTHER #2. (*spoken*) Now take a bowl of Jello. Any flavor
will do. Hold it real close to your sister's face and say:
   BROTHER #1. (*sings*)
DID YOU KNOW THAT JELLO IS REALLY ALIVE?
SEE HOW IT WIGGLES? THAT PROVES IT'S ALIVE.
(*SISTERS are getting convinced.*)

BROTHER #2.
SURE, IT'S DELICIOUS
BUT JELLO IS VICIOUS
AND SOMETIMES, WHEN KIDS TURN THEIR BACKS . . .
(*BROTHERS duck and hold up Jello, circling the bowls in the
   air like sharks.*)
ALL BROTHERS. (*spoken, lunging*)
IT ATTACKS!
(*The SISTERS scream.*)

ALL BROTHERS. (*beside themselves with glee*)
THAT'S HOW TO TORTURE YOUR SISTER.
LA-LA-LA-LA.
THAT'S HOW TO TORTURE HER GOOD.

DREAM UP NEW FORMS OF TORTURE.
BE CREATIVE. LET GO.
   BROTHER #1.
DROP A MOUSE DOWN HER SHIRT.
   BROTHER #2.
FILL HER LUNCHBOX WITH DIRT.
   BROTHER #3.
HOLD YOUR NOSE WHEN SHE SINGS.
   BROTHER #4.
USE HER TUB. LEAVE THE RINGS.
   BROTHER #1.
PAINT HER BLUE.
   BROTHER #2.
PAINT HER RED.
   BROTHER #3.
HIDE HER SHOE.
   BROTHER #4.
SHAVE HER HEAD.
   SISTERS.
STOP IT!
   BROTHERS.
STOP IT!
   SISTERS.
STOP IT!
   BROTHERS.
STOP IT!

SISTERS.
STAHHHHHHHHHHHHHHHHP!

BROTHERS.
THAT'S HOW TO TORTURE YOUR SISTER.
THAT'S HOW TO TORTURE HER —
SISTERS.
Stop it!
BROTHERS. (*mock sympathetic*) Awwwwwww . . .
HOW ARE YOU, FATS?
(*SISTERS whimper.*)
LOOK THERE, NOW THAT'S —
(*SISTERS whimper again.*)
HOW TO TORTURE YOUR
SIS — TER!

(*BROTHERS release spring-loaded snakes in SISTERS' faces. SISTERS scream. BROTHERS roar with laughter. Black out.*)

LESSON #18

PAULA removes previous title card to reveal "How to Look Forward to Your Birthday." She exits.
ANDY sits alone, C.S., calm and pleased with himself.

[MUSIC NO. 9: "THE BIRTHDAY SONG"]

(*NOTE: Unaffected simplicity is most effective here. It requires little or no movement about the stage. A fairly good singer is called for in order to sustain the long lines.*)

ANDY.
NEXT MONDAY IS MY BIRTHDAY,
IN CASE YOU HAVEN'T GUESSED.
AND ALL DAY LONG WE'RE GONNA CELEBRATE.
I COULDN'T EVEN TELL YA
WHICH PART I LOVE THE BEST,
'CAUSE EVERY PART IS SO DARN GREAT.

THE TINGLE-Y PART,
IT HAPPENS RIGHT AT THE START.
IT'S WHEN I WAKE WITH A SHOCK,
LOOK AT THE CLOCK
AND IT'S EIGHT
MINUTES TO FIVE.

THE WONDERFUL PART,
THAT'S WHEN I OPEN MY GIFTS.
AND EV'RY PRESENT I SEE
TURNS OUT TO BE WHAT I WANT . . .
OR PRACTIC'LY.

THE FUNNIEST PART IS THE PARTY,
WHEN ALL OF MY FRIENDS ARE HERE.
THE SORRIEST PART IS MY BEDTIME,
WHEN EV'RYTHING ENDS
UNTIL NEXT YEAR.

(*He stands and walks* DS.)

BUT HERE IS THE PART
THAT MAKES ME LAUGH IN MY HEART:
IT'S WHEN MY MOM AND MY DAD
TELL ME THEY'RE GLAD
I WAS BORN.

IT'S WHEN THEY CALL ME THE BIRTHDAY BOY,*
IT'S WHEN THEY TELL ME I BRING THEM JOY.

YES, THAT'S WHAT I LOVE,
THE CHANCE FOR ALL OF THE WORLD,
INCLUDING ME AND MY MOM AND MY DAD,
TO ALL BE GLAD
I WAS BORN.

(*Cross fade to* D.L.)

---

*If the song is to be performed by a girl, change this line to "the birthday girl"
and do not worry that it doesn't rhyme.

LESSON #19

BILLY stands in front of GEORGE as the reporter, and JOHN, who are at a table. On the table is a brown lunch bag.

BILLY. (*clicking a movie clapper board*) How to Eat Like a Child, Part 4. (*Exits.*)

JOHN. (*waving a chicken drumstick and chanting*) Roast chicken, boo; fried chicken, yay. Roast chicken, boo—

GEORGE. (*clearing his throat*) Excuse me. (*JOHN stops, realizing there's an audience. GEORGE puts on his reporter's voice.*) We're at the school cafeteria with John, who will show us how to eat a bag lunch. Where do you start?

JOHN. (*chanting again*) Roast chicken, boo; fried—

GEORGE. Yes, well, I mean after that. What else do you have to eat? Carrot sticks? (*He picks them up.*)

JOHN. (*taking them*) I put those here. (*He sticks one stick on top of each ear, like a pencil.*)

GEORGE. (*taken aback*) Oh. What about your hard-boiled egg?

JOHN. I peel it. (*does so and shows naked egg to GEORGE*) Then I cover it with dirty fingerprints (*does so*) and leave it on the cafeteria table.

GEORGE. (*more taken aback*) I see. What about your dessert?

JOHN. Oh, yes, my dessert. (*He holds up a cupcake.*) Actually I usually eat my cupcake first. Sometimes I even eat it on my way to school. Like this. (*He licks the frosting off.*) It's important to get as much frosting on your face as possible. (*demonstrates*)

GEORGE. I think you need a napkin.

JOHN. Kids don't use napkins. Kids use shirts. (*JOHN wipes his face with his hand, and his hand off on his shirt.*)

GEORGE. (*increasingly dismayed*) Is that all?

JOHN. Not quite. (*He blows air into his lunch bag and smashes the bag. GEORGE jumps.*) Then I have to spend the rest of lunch sitting with the little kids.

(*Black out.*)

[MUSIC NO. 9A: PLAYOFF]

Lesson #20

BRANDON removes previous title card to reveal "How to Act After Being Sent to your Room." *He exits.*
Lights up C.S., *which suggests a girl's bedroom. RACHEL storms on stage in a fury.*

[MUSIC NO. 10: "SAYONARA"]

(*NOTE: This song has a large repertoire of moods — fury, determination, stoicism, pathos and simple relief. In casting the role, look for someone with a natural tendency toward the over-dramatic. Think of it as an operatic aria.*)

RACHEL.
I HATE THEM.
(*She stamps her foot.*)
I HATE THEM.
(*She smashes her pillow.*)
I HATE THEM, I HATE THEM, I HATE THEM.
(*She throws herself down on her bed.*)

OKAY, I CUT MY BROTHER'S HAIR . . .
SHORT . . .
VERY . . .
FOR THAT THEY THROW ME INTO SOLITARY,
WITH NOTHING UP HERE BUT MY PRIVATE STER-E-
-O MEDIA CENTER TO KEEP ME DISTRACTED.
WELL, I THINK THEY OVER-REACTED.

(*She stands.*)
WHERE IS JUSTICE?
WHERE IS FAIR PLAY?
WHERE IS MY SUITCASE?
I'M RUNNING AWAY TONIGHT.

(*She gets out a small suitcase and starts to pack her dolls.*)

SINCE NOBODY LOVES ME
I'LL QUIETLY DROP OUT OF SIGHT.

(*pretending to write a note*)
DEAR PARENTS, I WON'T SEE YOU ANYMORE.
I TRIED FOR TEN YEARS BUT YOU WRECKED IT.
JUST LEAVE MY ALLOWANCE OUTSIDE THE DOOR.
AND FOUR TIMES A YEAR I'LL COME BY
    LATE AT NIGHT TO COLLECT IT.

SAYONARA!
GOOD-BYE FOR GOOD!
DON'T FEEL GUILTY,
(*accusingly*)
EVEN THOUGH YOU SHOULD.

(*with great sadness*)
TELL GRANDMA TO THINK OF ME NOW AND THEN.
TELL GIRL SCOUTS THAT I'VE RELOCATED.
TELL JUNIOR HIS HAIR WILL GROW OUT AGAIN.
(*suddenly furious again*)
I STILL THINK THAT HAIRDO'S
    THE BEST ONE I EVER CREATED.

SAYONARA!
THIS IS NO BLUFF!
GOOD-BYE FOREVER!
    BILLY. (*off-stage as "the father"*) Come on down for dinner,
dear.
    RACHEL. (*spoken*) Thank goodness. (*sung*)
I'VE SUFFERED ENOUGH!

(*Black out.*)

LESSON #21

REBECCA removes previous title card to reveal "How to Watch
    More Television." *She exits.*
DARIEN is D.R.

    DARIEN. Please, Mom, please. Just this once. I'll only ask
once. I promise, if you let me watch this show, I'll go to bed the
second it's over. I won't complain. I won't ask for a drink of

water. I won't ask for anything. Please. If you let me do this, I'll never ask you anything again. Never. Please, Mommy, please. You are the nicest mommy. You are the sweetest, nicest mommy. I promise I won't be cranky tomorrow. I promise I'll go to bed tomorrow at nine. Pleasepleaseplease. (*A beat.*)

Why not! Just give me a reason. I told you I'll be good. I told you I'll go to bed. Don't you believe me? Don't you trust me? Some mom — doesn't even trust her own kid. Look, I'll just close my eyes and listen. I won't even watch it! Oh, Mom, why can't I?

(*Segue to . . .*)

LESSON #22

ENTIRE COMPANY, except COREY, enters. Each has a pillow and blanket; some have stuffed animals and other bedtime gear. Some kids are pelting each other with pillows; some talk; some read; some chase each other.
Suddenly the action stops.

ALL. How to Go to Bed.

[MUSIC NO. 11: "WE REFUSE TO FALL ASLEEP"]*

(*Action resumes. MUSIC.*)

COREY. (*Off-stage as "the father;" at the sound of his voice, they freeze.*) I thought I told you kids to go to bed. (*MUSIC.*)
ALL. Okay, okay. We're going. (*MUSIC.*)
COREY. Well, make it snappy. (*They break from the freeze.*)

ARLENE. (*sings*)
THEY CAN FORCE US INTO OUR P-J'S.
THEY CAN FORCE US TO COUNT SHEEP.
THEY CAN FORCE US UNDER THE COVERS.
BUT THEY CAN'T FORCE US TO FALL ASLEEP.
ALL KIDS.
WE REFUSE TO FALL ASLEEP.
WE REFUSE TO FALL ASLEEP.

---

*Simple dance movement is called for: cool and hip during the verses, frantic and punky on the choruses.

WE'VE DECIDED ONE AND ALL
THAT WE'RE NEVER GONNA FALL
ASLEEP.

(*All the kids go crazy, running around, pelting each other, jumping up and down, rough-housing. MUSIC continues, until:*)

COREY. (*off-stage*) What's going on up there? (*They freeze at the sound of his voice. MUSIC.*)
   ALL. (*innocently*) Nothing. (*MUSIC.*)
   COREY. Well, turn out the lights. (*MUSIC.*)
   ALL. Okay.

(*Lights dim. One by one they turn on flashlights.*)

GEORGE and ARLENE.
WE'VE GOT BROWNIES. PLENTY OF KOOL-ADE.
WE'VE GOT MARS BARS FOR DESSERT.
WE'LL READ COMICS, LISTEN TO MUSIC,
EXCEPT FOR WHEN WE'RE ON DAD-ALERT.
   ANDY. Whoop-whoop-whoop! Dad-alert. Dad-alert.

(*All kids dive under the blankets. Pause. COREY enters and inspects all the beds suspiciously. He exits. Bedlam again.*)

ALL.
WE REFUSE TO FALL ASLEEP.
WE REFUSE TO FALL ASLEEP.
WE'VE DECIDED ONE AND ALL
THAT WE'RE NEVER GONNA FALL
ASLEEP.

WE'LL GREET THE SUN.
WE'LL WATCH IT RISE
OVER OUR BREAKFAST OF ESKIMO PIES.

SO IF YOUR BEDTIME'S AWFULLY EARLY,
IF YOUR DAY ENDS MUCH TOO SOON,
DO LIKE WE DO. MAKE IT A PARTY.
AND KEEP PLAYING BENEATH THE MOON.

(*Kids all link arms in solidarity.*)

WE REFUSE TO FALL ASLEEP.

GEORGE. (*ad lib as rock star,* C.S.)
WE ABSOLUTELY REFUSE.
ALL OTHER KIDS.
WE REFUSE TO FALL ASLEEP.
GEORGE.
WE REFUSE, WE REFUSE.
ALL.
WHEN WE'RE HAVING SUCH A BALL
WHY WOULD ANYBODY FALL
ASLEEP?

(*Some kids, too tired to continue, nod off to sleep. Others, fighting sleep, continue doggedly.*)

SEVEN KIDS.
WE REFUSE TO FALL ASLEEP.
WE REFUSE TO FALL ASLEEP.

(*Three more nod off.*)

FOUR KIDS.
THERE'S A MILLION WAYS TO STALL.
ONLY STUPID HEADS WOULD FALL
ASLEEP. (*They nod off.*)

BRANDON. (*the last one awake*)
I REFUSE TO FALL ASLEEP.
I REFUSE TO FALL ASLEEP.
THERE'S A MONSTER IN THE HALL.
I REFUSE TO FALL ASLEEP.
I REFUSE TO FALL ASLEEP.
I REFUSE TO . . . (*He yawns.*)
. . . SLEEP.
I RE . . . (*BRANDON is asleep.*)

(*After applause, PAULA pops up.*)

PAULA. Our Father, who art in heaven, hallowed be Thy name. Thy Kingdom come, Thy will be done, on earth as it is in heaven. Give us this day our daily bread, and forgive our trespasses as we forgive those who trespass against us. And lead us not into Penn Station, but deliver us from evil, for Thine is the Kingdom and the power and the glory for ever and ever.

RICKY. I wish there would be no war between anyone, anywhere.

ARLENE. I wish that Grandma would get well.

GEORGE. I wish I had a million dollars.

ALL. Amen!!

(*Segue to . . .*)

[MUSIC NO. 12: "LIKE A CHILD" (*Reprise*)]

GEORGE.
HERE IS OUR LAST LESSON.
ARLENE.
IT'S GOT THE MORAL IN IT.
GEORGE.
HOW YOU EAT STUFF ALL DEPENDS
ON HOW YOU FEEL THIS MINUTE.
SUNSHINE.
NOW YOU COULD SIT AND THINK ABOUT THE
MORAL . . .
RICKY.
. . . OR YOU COULD COME ALONG AND JOIN US,
RACHEL.
CLOWN AROUND THE PLAYGROUND,
PAULA.
JUMP AND BUMP YOUR NOGGIN,
ANDY.
TRIP AND RIP YOUR TROUSERS,
JOHN.
LOSE YOUR MITTEN,
DARIEN.
SKIN YOUR ELBOW,
ARLENE.
AND START TO CRY,
ALL.
AND, FIFTEEN SECONDS LATER,
FEEL SO HIGH,
ROAMIN' THROUGH THE WILD
LIKE A . . .
PAULA.
WE DO WHAT WE'VE GOT TO,
CHRISTY.
EVEN IF WE'RE NOT TO.

ALL.
LIKE A CHI-CHI-CHILD.
LIKE A CHI-CHI-CHILD!
YEAH!

[MUSIC NO. 13: BOWS]

Supplemental Lessons

(If desired, the following material may be inserted immediately after Lesson 15, and the subsequent Lessons renumbered.)

GEORGE. (*removing previous title card*) How to Behave at School.

(*Lights up* C.S. *RACHEL, PAULA, BILLY, REBECCA, KIMBERLY, and COREY deliver this lesson in spoken choral reading style or in a set that suggests a classroom.*)

PAULA. Arrive at school late. Explain that you are tardy because you couldn't find your shoe.

BILLY. As soon as the teacher turns to write on the blackboard, open your desk, pull out Mad Magazine and put it inside your language arts workbook. Read Mad Magazine while it looks as if you are reading language arts.

REBECCA. Chew a pencil.

PAULA. Pretend that your pencils are ships. Steer them around your desk and make them collide.

COREY. Then, pretending to play the drums, tap your desk with the pencil and when it's time to hit the cymbals, tap the head of the kid in front.

KIMBERLY. Click your pen.

RACHEL. Tell your teacher that you do not have your homework because your dog ate it.

BILLY. Deny that you are chewing gum and stick it on the roof of your mouth.

PAULA. Whisper. Stop when the teacher says,

RACHEL. (*as "the teacher"*) Would you like to go to the principal's office?

PAULA. Look at the clock.

REBECCA. When the teacher asks for a volunteer to take names while she goes out for a few minutes, raise your hand, shake it frantically, and shout . . .

COREY. Me, me, me, me, me, me, me.

REBECCA. You do not get chosen.

KIMBERLY. (*announcing*) What to do when your teacher is out of the classroom.

BILLY. Hold your nose and say . . .

PAULA. (*holding her nose*) Now class, behave.

RACHEL. Run to the front and draw your fingernails down the blackboard. Get your name taken.

BILLY. When a kid shoots a spitball and doesn't get his name taken, say—

COREY. How come you took my name and not his?

BILLY. Get his name taken.

RACHEL Smell something funny. Shriek—

COREY. Someone laid one, someone laid one, silent-but-deadly.

KIMBERLY. (*accusing COREY; gleeful*) He who smelt it, dealt it.

RACHEL. Wave hand in front of face. Crack up. Hold nose while each kid in the class also holds his nose and insists that it was another kid.

REBECCA. Yell, "She's coming."

KIMBERLY. And fall out of your chair just as the teacher returns.

REBECCA. Ask to sharpen your pencil.

BILLY. Ask to get a drink of water.

COREY. Ask to go to the bathroom. You can't hold it.

PAULA. Look at the clock.

ALL. Recess!

PAULA. (*stepping forward*) One of the best ways to spend recess is bragging.

[MUSIC: THE BRAG RAG]

BILLY. How to Brag.

(*Lights up on RICKY and JOHN, hanging around at recess.*)

RICKY.
I'M LEFT-HANDED.
JOHN.
I AM DOUBLE JOINTED.
(*He demonstrates.*)
RICKY.
I CAN SQUAT AND CRACK MY KNEES.
(*He does.*)
JOHN.
WELL, I CAN BURP ANYTIME I PLEASE.
RICKY.
OH, YEAH?
JOHN.
OH YEAH!

RICKY.
LET'S SEE!
(*JOHN burps long and loudly.*)
THAT'S NOTHING!
I BURP BETTER.
   JOHN.
I BURP BETTER!
   RICKY.
I BURP BETTER
THAN YOU COULD EVER BURP.

   JOHN.
WELL, I'VE GOT FILLINGS.
   RICKY.
I'VE HAD SEVEN STITCHES.
   JOHN.
GOT MY TONSILS IN A JAR.
   RICKY.
WELL, *I'VE* HAD SURGERY.
   JOHN.
WHERE'S THE SCAR?
   RICKY.
IT'S HEALED.
   JOHN.
THAT'S BULL!
   RICKY.
I SWEAR!
JUST CALL THE HOSPITAL.
THEY'LL TELL YOU
I'VE BEEN SICKER.
   JOHN.
I'VE BEEN SICKER!
   RICKY.
I'VE BEEN SICKER
THAN YOU COULD EVER BE.

   JOHN & RICKY. (*joined by entire COMPANY, if you wish*)
BRAG, BRAG, BRAG, BRAG, BRAG
DAY IN AND DAY OUT.
IF IT'S WORTH MENTIONING
IT'S CERTAINLY WORTH BRAGGIN' ABOUT.

RICKY.
MY JOKE'S DIRTY.
JOHN.
MY JOKE'S TEN TIMES DIRTIER.
RICKY.
MINE'S FROM PLAYBOY MAGAZINE.
JOHN.
WELL, MINE'S SO DIRTY THAT IT'S OBSCENE.
RICKY. (*interested*)
OH, YEAH?
JOHN. (*smugly*)
IT'S GREAT!
RICKY.
LET'S HEAR.
(*JOHN whispers in RICKY's ear. RICKY cracks up. Then . . .*)
I don't get it.
JOHN.
BOY, YOU'RE STUPID.
RICKY.
I'M NOT STUPID.
JOHN.
YOU'RE THE STUPIDEST KID
I'VE EVER SEEN.

RICKY.
WELL, I'M A GREAT BRAGGER.
JOHN.
I BRAG EVEN BETTER.
RICKY.
I CAN BRAG ABOUT GIRLS I'VE KISSED.
JOHN.
AND THAT'S A TRICK WHEN THEY DON'T EXIST.
RICKY.
YES THEY DO!

JOHN & RICKY. (*with COMPANY, optional*)
BRAG, BRAG, BRAG, BRAG, BRAG
DAY IN AND DAY OUT.
IF IT'S WORTH MENTIONING,
IT'S CERTAINLY WORTH BRAGGIN' ABOUT.
RICKY.
SO WE'LL KEEP BRAGGIN' . . .

JOHN. (*with COMPANY, optional*)
WE'LL KEEP BRAGGIN' . . .
RICKY.
BRAG, BRAG, BRAGGIN' . . .
JOHN. (*with COMPANY, optional*)
BRAG, BRAG, BRAGGIN' . . .
RICKY.
I BRAG BETTER . . .
JOHN.
I BRAG MUCH BETTER . . .
RICKY.
I BRAG MUCH, MUCH BETTER . . .
JOHN.
I BRAG VERY MUCH . . .
JOHN & RICKY. (*with COMPANY, optional*)
BETTER THAN ANYONE ELSE
COULD EVER BRAG.
JOHN.
SAYS YOU!

JOHN & RICKY. (*announcing*) How to Go Home from School.

(*JOHN and RICKY now begin talking together quietly as EN-TIRE COMPANY enters s.l., if not already on stage, also chatting among themselves. All move toward stage right exit. BRANDON enters last, tagging several paces behind.*)

RACHEL. (*chanting*) Step on a crack, break your mother's back.
ARLENE. (*chanting*) Step on a line, break your mother's spine.
PAULA. Pull leaves off hedges.
DARIEN & BILLY. Kick a rock as you walk.
COREY. Avoid quicksand.
CHRISTY. Jump up—grab a branch of a tree.
PAULA. Run—you are being chased by red ants.

(*Now rapidly.*)

REBECCA. Ring the bell.
SUNSHINE. Hit the knocker.
ANDY. Slam the door.
KIMBERLY. Shout:

ALL. (*shouting*) "Hey, Mom, it's me."

(*Suddenly BRANDON bolts from the back of the crowd toward the* s.r. *exit.*)

BRANDON. (*as he exits*) And race to the bathroom.

(*Black out.*)

SONG NOTES

Although HOW TO EAT LIKE A CHILD does not require any choreography, four numbers ("Like A Child," "Say Yes," "How To Torture Your Sister" and "We Refuse to Fall Asleep") would be enhanced by some simple dance steps (see notes on individual songs). Regarding performance style, simple and truthful is usually best. When in doubt, a child should imagine himself or herself in the same situation in real life and work from that. Regarding gender, the only song that is truly gender-specific is "How To Torture Your Sister." It makes no difference whether a girl or a boy performs "Why Should A Kid Have To Walk," "Waiting, Waiting," or "The Birthday Song," but "Sayonara" feels right for a girl, "Say Yes" for two boys. Use your discretion.

SET NOTES

HOW TO EAT LIKE A CHILD can be performed in almost any space using a very simple set. Lighting is not necessary, though it obviously adds theatricality. The open stage should suggest a child's environment. Downstage left stands an easel. On it are placed all the title cards, which are removed and carried offstage, one by one, in the course of the play. Ten or twelve lightweight cubes (about 2′ × 2′ and painted bright colors) are placed in various configurations to suggest the "furniture": three groups of three cubes each for the girls' beds in "I Feel Sick;" two groups of two cubes each for the car seats in "How to Ride;" a stack of two or three cubes for the rostrum in "How to Express an Opinion;" two or three cubes for the bench in "Waiting, Waiting;" four isolated single cubes for the sisters' telephone seats in "How to Torture Your Sister;" various groupings to suggest the bed, bookshelves, and writing table of the girls' bedroom in "Sayonara;" groups suggesting beds of various lengths and levels for "We Refuse to Fall Asleep;" single cubes for classroom seats in "How to Behave at School," etc. Some of the cubes could be hollow (like a milk crate); some could be oblong. The cast members should change the cubes from one configuration to the next in full view of the audience. A simple jungle gym of climbing equipment might be useful for staging, but is not necessary. A backdrop (possibly a mural drawn by the kids themselves) is optional, as is the spotlight for the opening sequence.

COSTUME NOTES

Kids should wear their own clothes—play clothes like jeans, sweatshirts and T-shirts. Nothing too cute and nothing dressy. No fancy hairdos. They should look the way they do every day.

When a kid plays "father" or "mother," he or she can add a detail to their outfits to indicate. For instance, as the song "How to Understand Your Parents" begins, Kimberly (the mother) can tie on an apron and Darien (the father) can slip on a suit jacket. The mother in "How to Stay Home From School" can wear a bathrobe or very grown-up eyeglasses. Corey, the father, in "How to Go to Bed," should have a tie on over his T-shirt.

PROPERTY LIST

Easel
Title Cards
  How to Eat Like a Child (on top of stack as play begins)
  How to Stay Home From School
  How to Ride in a Car
  How to Practice the Violin
  How to Express an Opinion
  How to Beg for a Dog
  How to Play
  How to Understand Your Parents
  How to Deal With Injustice
  How to Hang up the Telephone
  How to Wait
  How to Torture Your Sister
  How to Look Forward to Your Birthday
  How to Act After Being Sent to Your Room
  How to Watch More Television

Prologue
  telephone
  book
  yoyo
  an orange cut into quarters
  chewing gum

Lesson #1
  movie clapper board with "How to Eat" written on it
  hand-held microphone or a facsimile
  plate of mashed potatoes, cup of gravy, peas
  package of French fries (McDonald's style)

Lesson #2
  3 blankets, one per child

Lesson #4
  telephone

Lesson #5
  violin and bow
  music stand

a music book
metronome

Lesson #6
  podium

Lesson #7
  pair of cocker spaniel ears (suggestion: earmuffs altered to
    look like dog's ears)

Lesson #8
  a drinking glass (as for juice or milk)

Lesson #10
  telephone

Lesson #11
  movie clapper board with "How to Eat" written on it
  large paper cup (filled with milk) and straw
  hand-held microphone or facsimile

Lesson #12
  broom and/or duster

Lesson #13
  two telephones

Lesson #14
  kid's winter parka
  backpack
  thermos

Lesson #15
  movie clapper board with "How to Eat" written on it
  box of animal crackers
  hand-held microphone or facsimile

Lesson #16
  telephone

Lesson #17
  four telephones

four jelly doughnuts
four bowls of Jello
four spring-loaded snakes in a can (open the can and out
   it pops; sometimes labelled "Peanut Brittle")

Lesson #19
   movie clapper board with "How to Eat" written on it
   brown paper lunch bag
   chicken drumstick
   carrot sticks
   hard-boiled egg
   cupcake
   hand-held microphone or a facsimile

Lesson #20
   small suitcase
   pillow
   a few stuffed animals

Lesson #22
   pillows, one per child
   flashlights, one per child
   blankets, one per child
   a few stuffed animals